TWO
GIRLS
CAN!

by Keiko Narahashi

Margaret K. McElderry Books

To Joy, my best girlfriend
—K.N.

Margaret K. McElderry Books
An imprint of Simon & Schuster Children's Publishing Division
1230 Avenue of the Americas
New York, New York 10020

Copyright © 2000 by Keiko Narahashi

Book design by Ann Bobco
The text of this book is set in VAG Rounded BT.
The illustrations were rendered in watercolor.

Printed in China

10 9 8 7 6 5 4 3 2 1

Library of Congress Cataloging-in-Publication Data
Narahashi, Keiko.
Two girls can! / Keiko Narahashi.—1st ed.
p.   cm.
Summary: Two girls celebrate all the things that friends can do together.
ISBN 0-689-82618-4
[1. Friendship—Fiction.] I. Title.
PZ7.N158Tw   2000   [E]—dc21   98-45301

Two girls can

hold
hands,

give bear hugs,

be best friends.

Two girls can

stay dry,

or get wet,

and dry again.

Two girls can

fly a kite,

or dig a hole,

then make a tunnel

and meet in the middle.

Two girls can

get
really,
really
mad,

then make up

and be brave together.

Two girls can

leapfrog,

seesaw,

tug-of-war.

Two girls can

hide,

spy,

and surprise!

Two girls can

pretend they're twins

or be real twins

or a big and little sister.

Two girls can

share a treat,

share a joke,

share with a friend.

Two girls can

climb a wall,

climb a tree,

and reach a high-up branch.

Two girls can

be
quiet
together,

sing a song together,

make a great big noise together.

Two girls can

dance!

but so can three—

and four,

and five.

Come on, everybody,

let's dance!